To:

From:

for Aaron,
my best friend and my biggest helper

Copyright © 2007 Hallmark Licensing, Inc.

Published by Hallmark Books,
a division of Hallmark Cards, Inc.,
Kansas City, MO 64141
Visit us on the Web at www.Hallmark.com.

Editorial Director: Todd Hafer
Editor: Theresa Trinder
Art Director: Kevin Swanson
Designer: Mary Eakin
Production Artist: Dan Horton

ISBN 978-1-59530-160-4

BOK6074

Printed and bound in China

Rodney
the
Reindeer

The **BIG** Story of Santa's **LITTLEST** Helper

Way up at the North Pole, all the reindeer were excited!
After all, it was the best day of the year to be a reindeer.
It was Christmas Eve!

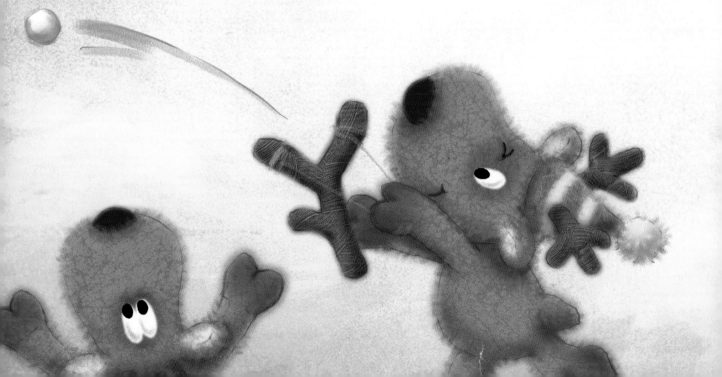

Reindeer Games

And while all the grown-up reindeer
were busy preparing for Santa's flight,
all the little reindeer were competing in
the Reindeer Games. There was the
Wreath Toss, the Snowball Slingshot,
and everyone's favorite game, the
Six-Legged Race.

The Games were a North Pole
tradition, and every little
reindeer joined in.

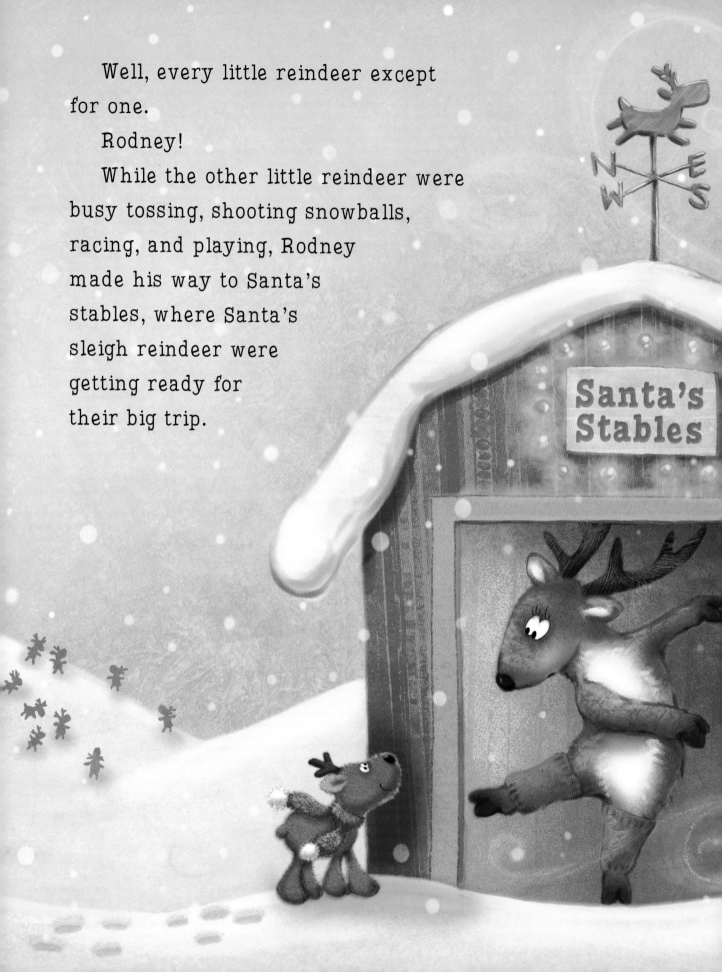

Well, every little reindeer except for one.

Rodney!

While the other little reindeer were busy tossing, shooting snowballs, racing, and playing, Rodney made his way to Santa's stables, where Santa's sleigh reindeer were getting ready for their big trip.

Santa's Stables

"Hi, Dancer! Can I help you get ready for Christmas?" Rodney asked.

"Sorry, Rodney. You're just too little. Why don't you go outside and play?"

"Hmm . . ." thought Rodney. He did like playing games. But what he really wanted was to help everyone get ready for Christmas. It was his favorite day of the year!

"I don't want to play," Rodney said. "I want to help!"

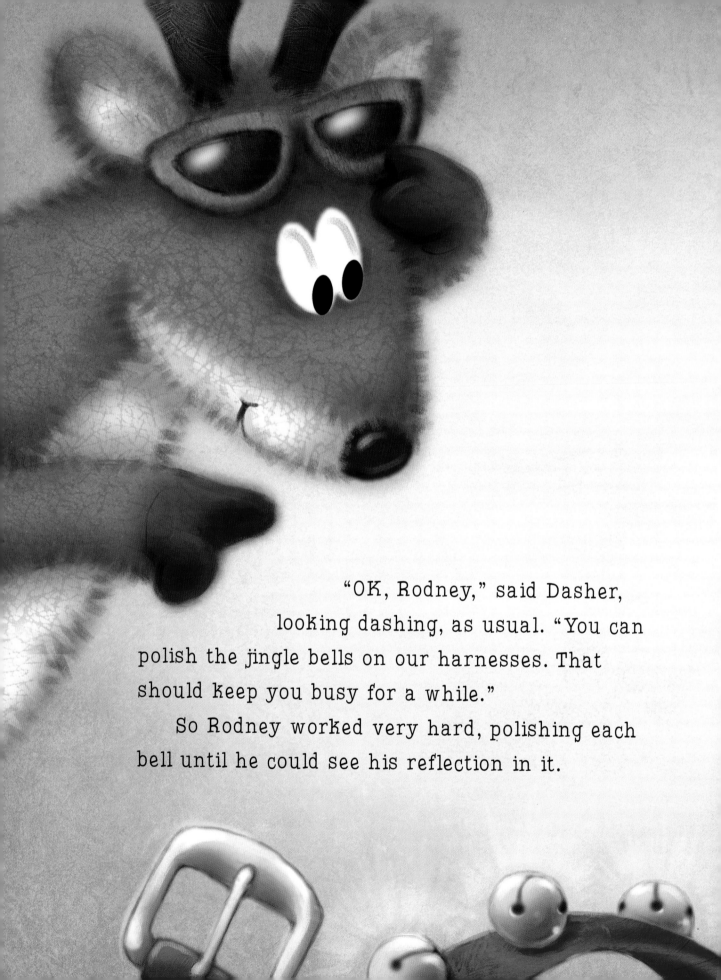

"OK, Rodney," said Dasher, looking dashing, as usual. "You can polish the jingle bells on our harnesses. That should keep you busy for a while."

So Rodney worked very hard, polishing each bell until he could see his reflection in it.

While he worked, he imagined he was one of Santa's sleigh reindeer with his own harness of shiny, jingling bells.

"All done!" Rodney said with pride. "What else can I do?"

"Why don't you go see Santa's elves?" asked Cupid, as she put her makeup on. "We have to get ready to fly!"

So Rodney went to Santa's workshop.
Everywhere he looked, there was
something to see. Mountains of toys!
Huge sheets of wrapping paper! Giant spools
of ribbon! And enormous bags
overflowing with presents!
All the elves were busy,
busy, busy! Surely they
could use some help . . .

Rodney tapped Pickles the Elf on the shoulder.
He looked like he was in charge. "Psst . . . Pickles!
Can I help?"

"Aaack! You scared me, Rodney! And no, you're too
little! And we're too busy! Why haven't you joined in
the Reindeer Games?"

"I don't want to play games," Rodney said sadly.
"I want to help."

"OK, OK!" Pickles said. "But BE CAREFUL! An elf's work is very serious business. If any of these presents gets mixed up, there are going to be some very sad boys and girls on Christmas morning."

So Rodney worked (very carefully!) beside Santa's elves.

He taped!

He tied!

And he watched every single present make its way down a long assembly line into the exact right giant bag.

When all the gifts were wrapped and
bagged, Rodney was jumping with excitement.
"We're done! What else can I do?"

But the elves were exhausted.

"Why don't you go see if Mrs.
Claus needs help with the sleigh?"
asked a very tired Pickles.
"We need a break!"

So Rodney went to Santa's garage, where the North Pole penguins were just starting to load the presents into the sleigh.

Rodney had never been this close to Santa's
sleigh before. It was beautiful!

"Mrs. Claus, ma'am," he said nervously, "can
I . . . may I . . . help, please?"

"I'm so sorry, Rodney. But you're too little to lift
such heavy bags. Plus, it's getting awfully windy
and icy out here! Why don't you go back inside the
workshop and get warm?"

"But I really want to help!" Rodney pleaded.

"All right, Rodney, let me
see . . . Santa's already made his
list and checked it twice. But why don't you
check it a third time? Make sure every child's
present is in the right bag, headed to the right place."

Mrs. Claus handed Rodney Santa's OFFICIAL LIST.
This was very serious business!

So present by present, bag by bag, Rodney checked
and checked until he had checked off
every name on Santa's list.

When he was finally done,
Rodney handed the list back to
Mrs. Claus. "What else can I do?"
he asked eagerly.

"The presents have all been loaded!"
Mrs. Claus replied. "That means it's
nearly time for takeoff. Now, quick,
Rodney! Run out and see!"

At the same time every year, Santa's eight great
reindeer pull his sleigh, piled high with toys, all the way
from his garage, down the entire length of Main Street
to the very edge of town, where it takes off for its flight
around the world.

Rodney watched and waited . . . until
Santa's reindeer appeared, two at a time,
with their harnesses of shining, jingling
bells. And then . . . there was Santa!
    The frosty wind blew his bristly
white beard and made his
plump cheeks as rosy as
peppermint candies.

Then, all of a sudden, over the cheers of the crowd came a great KER-CHUNK! Santa's sleigh struck a piece of ice in the path.

The big bags of presents bounced out of the sleigh, split open, and scattered boxes and bows all over the snowy ground.

Santa's list flew out of his pocket, swirled in the wind, and flew up, up, up . . .

. . . and away.

Main Street grew very quiet. The reindeer stood as still as statues. The elves bit their fingernails. The penguins hid their eyes. Santa looked at Mrs. Claus. Mrs. Claus looked at Santa.

"Oh, Santa!" she cried. "What a mess! Without
your list, how will you know what presents go where?
All those poor boys and girls will be so disappointed
if they don't get the gifts they asked for! And they've
been so good all year . . ."

Just then, a little, cheerful voice came from the very silent crowd.

"Mrs. Claus! Santa! I can help!"

"No, Rodney, you can't help," said Mrs. Claus.
"Not this time."

"But I can!" he said. "Because I know where
the presents go! I helped the elves wrap every one!
I sorted them into the bags! I triple-checked
Santa's list! I remember!

"That one's for Sarah! In Pleasanton!
It's a book! And that's for Peter! In
Riverside! It's a red race car!"

"Well, Rodney, it looks like you
worked very hard today," Santa
chuckled. "Would you like to
help one more time?"

Before Rodney could even
nod his head, Santa scooped
him up into the sleigh.
And the reindeer began
to trot, then gallop,
then race with all
their might down
Main Street.

Then suddenly, magically, the ground disappeared below them. Rodney was high above town. Santa's stables, workshop, and garage were tiny specks in a field of snow.

Rodney was flying!

Together they flew from roof to
roof, neighborhood to neighborhood,
country to country. Thanks to all his hard
work that day, Rodney was able to tell Santa
exactly where to go.

With Rodney's help, Santa delivered Mason's
model train, Brian's art set, Riley's roller skates,
Joshua's fishing pole . . . and thousands more!
He went down every chimney of every house
until every present in every bag was delivered.

"That's it, Santa!" Rodney shouted. "We're
finished! We did it!"

"Actually, there's one more present left," said Santa with a wink.

He reached his big gloved hand into his fuzzy coat pocket and pulled out a little box with a big green bow. And inside it was a shiny silver jingle bell—just like the ones Santa's sleigh reindeer wore.

To: Rodney
From: Santa

"It's for you, Rodney . . . my littlest helper."

Did you enjoy Rodney's big story?
Are you a little helper?
We'd love to hear from you!

Please mail us a letter:
Book Feedback
Mail Drop 215
2501 McGee Street
Kansas City, MO 64108

Or e-mail:
booknotes@hallmark.com